THE GHOST
WITH
THE HALLOWEEN HICCUPS

BY STEPHEN MOOSER
illustrated by
TOMIE DE PAOLA

AN EASY-READ STORY BOOK
FRANKLIN WATTS | NEW YORK | LONDON | 1977

For Mom and Dad

Library of Congress Cataloging in Publication Data

Mooser, Stephen.
  The ghost with the Halloween hiccups.

  (An Easy-read story book)
  SUMMARY: The lead in the Halloween play has
the hiccups and none of the townspeople's remedies
work.
  [1. Hiccups—Fiction.   2. Halloween—Fiction]
I. De Paola, Thomas Anthony.   II. Title.
PZ7.M78817Gh   [E]   77-6271
ISBN 0-531-01316-2

R.L. 2.0 Spache Modified Formula
EDL Core Vocabulary

9

Mr. Penny loved Halloween.

He was always in the Halloween play.

This year he was going to be the ghost.

On Halloween Mr. Penny
headed for town.

He met Bert and Laura along the way.

"Happy HICCUP Halloween."

"Oh my," said Laura.

"You have the hiccups."

"All HICCUP day," said Mr. Penny.

"That's too bad," said Bert.

"It's worse than HICCUP bad,"
said Mr. Penny.

"How can I play HICCUP a ghost
with hiccups?"

"What you need is a big drink of water,"
said Laura.

"Please, bring me some HICCUP water,"
said Mr. Penny. "The sooner I get rid
of these hiccups, the HICCUP better."

Laura gave Mr. Penny a glass of water.

Then he held his breath and waited.

Ten seconds went by.

He didn't hiccup once.

"That did it!" he said. "My hiccups
are HIC CUP HIC CUP HIC CUP!"
Bert sighed. "I'm sorry," he said.
"Maybe you can get rid of them in town."

Mr. Penny hiccuped into town.

"Hello Ms. HICCUP Gates," said Mr. Penny.

"How are you HICCUP today?"

"I'm fine, but you sound terrible,"
said Ms. Gates.

"I HICCUP must get over the hiccups.
I have to be in HICCUP the play."

"Hiccups are easy to fix," said Ms. Gates.

"All you have to do is put a paper hat
on your head. Then you sing a song."

So Mr. Penny put a paper hat on his head.
He tried to sing, "Row, row HIC CUP your
boat, gently down HIC CUP the stream."
That was as far as he could get.

"Do you have any more ideas?"
asked Mr. Penny.

Ms. Gates was out of ideas.

But Mr. Brown thought he could help.

"Tickle his nose," he said.

Ms. Gates found a feather.
She tickled Mr. Penny's nose.
" HIC CUP! AH-CHOO!" sneezed Mr. Penny.
" HIC CUP! AH-CHOO! HIC CUP!"

Mr. Penny started to cry.
"Now I have the AH-CHOO sneezes
as well as the HIC CUP hiccups."

"What am I HICCUP going to do?"
wondered Mr. Penny.
He went on down the road.
"The play starts HICCUP in an hour."

Then Mr. Penny saw Mayor Bell.

"I have good news," said the mayor.

"Everyone is coming to the play."

"I have HIC CUP bad news," said Mr. Penny.

"I can't be in the HIC CUP play.

I have the HIC CUP hiccups."

"But you have to be in it," said the mayor.

"Try hopping around on one foot," she said.

"Maybe you can shake those hiccups out."

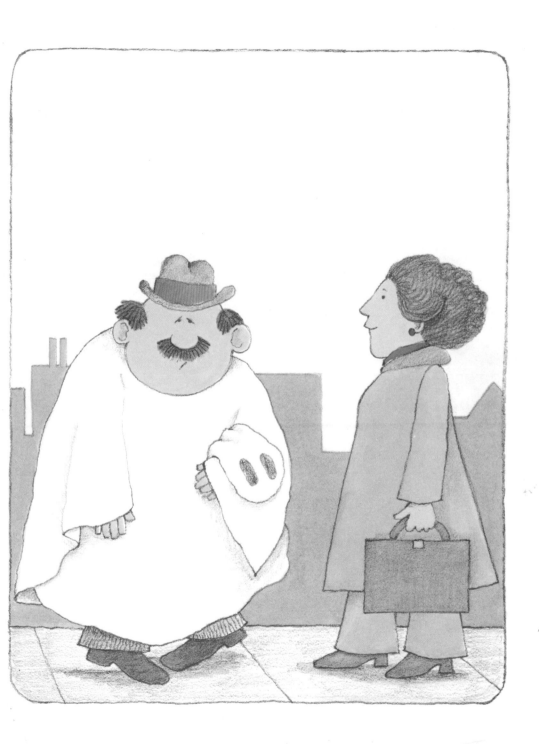

Mr. Penny started to hop.

Every time he came down he hiccuped.

"Why don't you stand on your head?"
asked the policeman.
"I'll HIC CUP try it," said Mr. Penny.
"I'll do HIC CUP anything."

Mr. Penny stood on his head.
"This doesn't HICCUP work," he said.
"This just makes my HICCUP face red."

As it grew later Mr. Penny tried everything.
"Quack like a duck," said the butcher.
So Mr. Penny tried quacking like a duck.
But QUACK, HIC CUP, QUACK, HIC CUP,
QUACK was the best he could do.

"Try barking," said the dog catcher.
"I've never seen a dog with the hiccups."
"BARK, HICCUP, BARK, HICCUP, BARK,"
hiccuped Mr. Penny.

Mr. Penny shook his head sadly.

Mr. Penny went to a corner of the park.

He put a paper hat on his head.

Then he stood on his head.

"I'll give it one HICCUP last try," he said.

"One of the HICCUP things should work.

QUACK, HICCUP, BARK, HICCUP,

QUACK, HICCUP, BARK, HICCUP!"

The town clock said seven.

"I'll have to HIC CUP HIC CUP tell everyone
to go HIC CUP home," he said.
"I'm afraid they will be HIC CUP mad."

He crossed Mill Road. Then Mr. Penny
stopped. His hair stood on end.
It was a hairy bat and a dragon.

"HIC CUP bats and HIC CUP dragons!"
screamed Mr. Penny. "HIC CUP help!"
He yelled, "run for your HIC CUP lives."

The monsters ran after Mr. Penny.

"Help HIC CUP, help HIC CUP police," shouted Mr. Penny. He was so scared he jumped right out of his shoes.

"Please don't hurt me," he begged.

"Mr. Penny, it's only me," said the bat, taking off her mask.

"And me," said the dragon. "We just wanted to trick you for Halloween."

Mr. Penny sighed and shook his head.
"It's just that I was so upset by my hiccups
that . . ." Suddenly, Mr. Penny stopped.

"My hiccups are gone! You scared them
out of me. Now I can be in the play,"
smiled Mr. Penny. "Your trick has
turned out to be a Halloween treat."

And Mr. Penny was the best ghost ever.